by Dayle Ann Dodds * pictures by Sachiko Yoshikawa

Dial Books for Young Readers

New York

To Kayli, full of sunshine
—D.D.

To Kinu, Dad, Mom, Nancy,
Wayne, and all my friends
—S.Y.

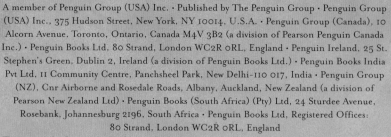

DIAL BOOKS FOR YOUNG READERS

A member of Penguin Group (USA) Inc. · Published by The Penguin Group · Penguin Group (USA) Inc., 375 Hudson Street, New York, NY 10014, U.S.A. · Penguin Group (Canada), 10 Alcorn Avenue, Toronto, Ontario, Canada M4V 3B2 (a division of Pearson Penguin Canada Inc.) · Penguin Books Ltd, 80 Strand, London WC2R 0RL, England · Penguin Ireland, 25 St. Stephen's Green, Dublin 2, Ireland (a division of Penguin Books Ltd.) · Penguin Books India Pvt Ltd, 11 Community Centre, Panchsheel Park, New Delhi-110 017, India · Penguin Group (NZ), Cnr Airborne and Rosedale Roads, Albany, Auckland, New Zealand (a division of Pearson New Zealand Ltd) · Penguin Books (South Africa) (Pty) Ltd, 24 Sturdee Avenue, Rosebank, Johannesburg 2196, South Africa · Penguin Books Ltd, Registered Offices: 80 Strand, London WC2R 0RL, England

Manufactured in China on acid-free paper
Text set in Mrs Eaves Roman · Designed by Teresa Kietlinski
1 3 5 7 9 10 8 6 4 2
LIBRARY OF CONGRESS CATALOGING-IN-PUBLICATION DATA
Dodds, Dayle Ann. Hello, sun! /
by Dayle Ann Dodds; pictures by Sachiko Yoshikawa.
p.   cm.   Summary: A young child must change clothes many times
as the weather goes from sunny to cloudy to rainy to snowy.
ISBN 0-8037-2895-6 [1. Weather—Fiction. 2. Clothing and dress—Fiction. 3. Stories in rhyme.]
I. Yoshikawa, Sachiko, ill. II. Title. PZ8.3.D645 He 2005   [E]—dc21   2002015605
The art was created using acrylics and pastel on watercolor paper.
Special thanks to Namiko Rudi and Kana Suzuki—S.Y.

HELLO, SUN,

cheerful and light.
These **PANTS** and **SHIRT**
will be just right.

Now I'm dressed and ready to go.
I open the door, but then . . .

UH-OH!

HELLO, CLOUDS,

fluffy and gray.
A **SWEATER** is better
to wear this day.

Now I'm dressed and ready to go.
I open the door, but then . . .

UH-OH!

HELLO, WIND,

chilly and snappy.
A **SCARF** and **JACKET**
will make me happy.

Now I'm dressed and ready to go.
I open the door, but then . . .

UH-OH!

HELLO, RAIN,

drippy and wet.
My **RAINCOAT** and **BOOTS**
will help, I bet.

Now I'm dressed and ready to go.
I open the door, but then . . .

UH-OH!

HELLO, SNOW,

white as kittens.
I think I'll need
my **COAT** and **MITTENS**.

Now I'm dressed and ready, and so,
I open the door and . . .

OFF
I GO!

and build a snowman round and plump.

My day is done
and yet I see,
one last friend
still waits for me.

HELLO, MOON,

jolly and bright.
You light my way
on this dark night,

and tell me that it's time to go.

I close my door to

MOON

and SNOW

and RAIN

and WIND

and CLOUDS

and SUN,

thankful for this day of fun.

And now my **PAJAMAS**
are just right.
I climb in bed and say . . .